This one is for Jan Berrien Berends
Beloved Number One Son of mine
and Best Big Brother of the other
With all my love   P.B.B.

To our New One   B.S.

A bird flew into the barnyard.
"I heard," said the bird.
"I heard..."

"What?" asked all the animals.
"What did you hear?"

"I heard," said the bird,
"that there's a NEW ONE coming."

Soon the barnyard was bustling
with the news.
Everyone began asking,
"What is the NEW ONE going to be?"

They asked the duck,
"Is the NEW ONE a duckling?"
But the duck said, "No."

They asked the pig,
"Is the NEW ONE a piglet?"
But the pig said, "No."

They asked the goose
and the hare.

They asked the mouse
and the mare.

They asked here
and there
and everywhere.

But everybody said, "No."

"How do you know
there's a NEW ONE coming?"
said the animals all together.

"I heard," said the bird.
"How?" said the cow.
"When?" said the hen.
"Where?" said the mare.
"In the house?"
   squeaked the mouse.

Just then a little boy
came out. "What's going on?"
he asked.
"Well," the animals told him,
"it's about the NEW ONE."
"I heard," said the bird.

"How?" said the cow.
"When?" said the hen.
"Where?" said the mare.
"In the house?"
squeaked the mouse.

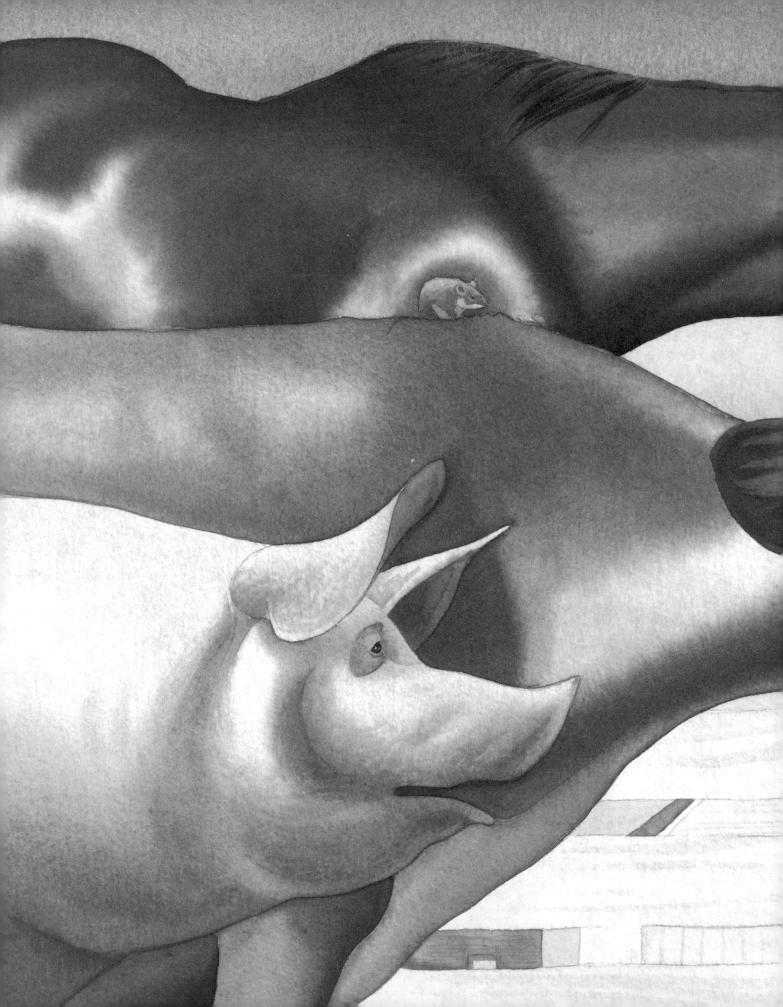

"Yes," said the little boy.

"YES, WHAT?" shouted
all the animals.

"Yes," said the little boy,
"the NEW ONE is in the house.
And if you'll be very quiet,
I'll let you see him."

"Ooooh!" cried the animals
all together.

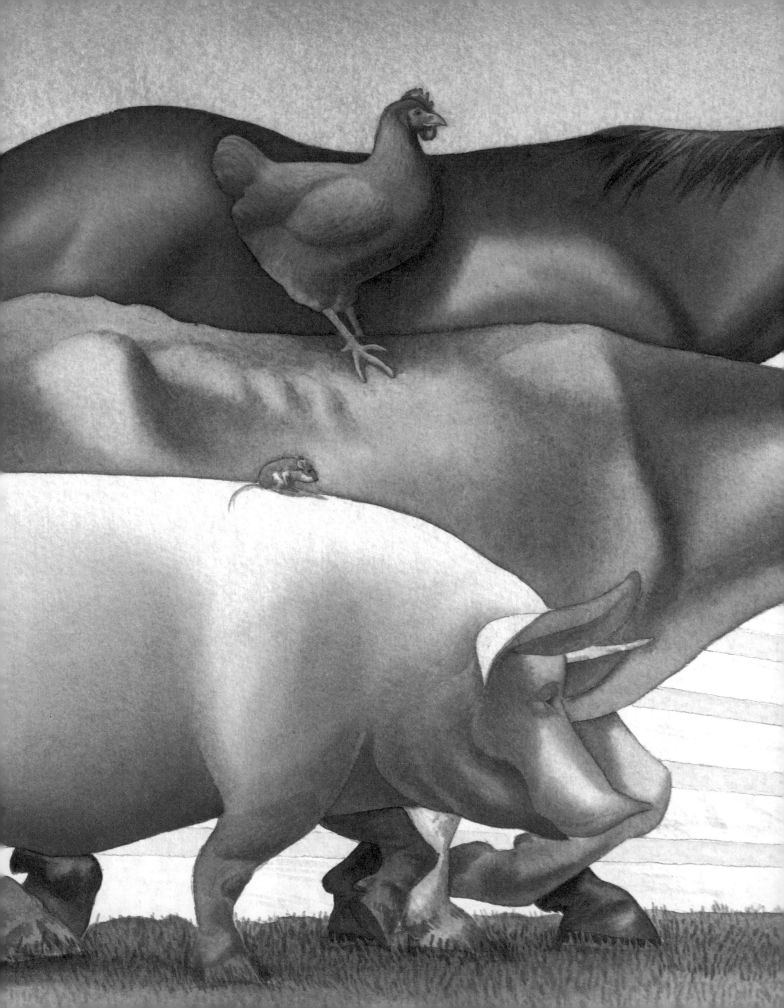

Then, very quietly, the little boy led the animals to the house. And, very quietly, they all tiptoed to the window and looked inside.

"It's a new baby," the little boy whispered.

"My word!" said the bird.
"And how!" said the cow.
"Of course," said the horse.

"I declare!"
said the hare.